Poetry Anthology
Warang Writers' World

W. J. Manares, et. al.

Ukiyoto Publishing

All global publishing rights are held by

Ukiyoto Publishing

Published in 2023

Content Copyright © W. J. Manares, et. al.

ISBN 9789360163976

*All rights reserved.
No part of this publication may be reproduced, transmitted, or stored in a retrieval system, in any form by any means, electronic, mechanical, photocopying, recording or otherwise, without the prior permission of the publisher.*

The moral rights of the authors have been asserted.

This is a work of fiction. Names, characters, businesses, places, events, locales, and incidents are either the products of the author's imagination or used in a fictitious manner. Any resemblance to actual persons, living or dead, or actual events is purely coincidental.

This book is sold subject to the condition that it shall not by way of trade or otherwise, be lent, resold, hired out or otherwise circulated, without the publisher's prior consent, in any form of binding or cover other than that in which it is published.

www.ukiyoto.com

To Balagtas & Bukowski

Paunang Salita

UNANG nabuo ang chat group na Warang Writers' World, phenomenal ang datingan, kasi, sa isang iglap maraming mga writer ang nakiisa sa layunin ng pangkat. Nagkaroon ng identity, tuluyang isinilang ang WARANG PUBLICATION HOUSE.

Hindi pa doon natapos ang pagsibol, iniluwal ng WPH ang mahigit sa sampung team na batay sa genre. Nangasim, naglihi at isinilang ng bawat kasapi ang kanilang obra, mga obrang hindi namimili ng henerasyon para basahin, mga akdang kaakibat ang pangako, alay sa reading community na ibibigay ang hilig, habang nanginginig, ihahandog ang takot, habang nangangatog, kakantiin ang guni-guni, hahamon sa kahinaan at susubok sa katatagan.

Kodus WARANG Writers, here is it now, the realization of our perseverance, the fruit of our sharing, and our dream before, now in reality.

Kris S. Alarde

Warang Adviser

Warm-Up Message

Dear Readers and Fellow Enthusiasts,

I am thrilled to share with you that this project has come to fruition. Do you know that this has been one of our dreams—to create and publish a physical book of our works? The group was formed on July 6, and on that same day, we decided to embark on this project. Our decision was swift, driven by a sense of urgency and excitement. And now, here we are. Perhaps it is because of the incredible individuals I have the privilege of working with, those who believed in each other and placed their trust in our collective vision.

I would like to extend my heartfelt congratulations to my comrades for taking the first step towards our dream. Your dedication and commitment have brought us this far. And to all of you who have joined us on this journey, I want to extend my warmest greetings. Thank you for being a part of these moments.

With heartfelt appreciation,

KOFFEEE (the one who started it all)

Contents

Introduction	1
Cool Or...	3
Diyona Ng Bahaghari	5
Broken Crayons	6
Colors Of Your Love	7
Kulay Ng Pag-ibig	9
Hue	11
Makulay Na Pagkabigo	13
Melancholy	15
Mutiny in Mt. Everest	16
The Covenant Bow	18
Sa Iyong Piling	19
Kapus-Palad	20
Bahaghari	22
The Colors	24
The Storm of Hope	26
Panahon	28
Nosibalasi	30

Introduction

The 1st Warang Poetry Anthology invites readers on a captivating poetic journey through the vast spectrum of human emotions and experiences. This compilation artfully weaves together diverse poems, each a shimmering gem in its own right, crafted by master wordsmiths of our time.

W. J. Manares | Marvin Wrighttee | KwiinMartha | Kristi June | Cherselle | Rhemaveal S. Bonifacio | Haya Jhie | ROSEANDTULIPS31 | ziniriya | DManunulat | Christian Dave Amada

From the tender innocence of first love to the searing pain of heartbreak, these verses explore the raw depths of human connections. Joyous celebrations of nature's beauty entwine with contemplative reflections on life's impermanence, reminding us to cherish every moment. Amidst the verses, dark shadows cast by grief, war, and loss are bravely confronted, fostering empathy and understanding.

Editors: Marvin Wrighttee & W. J. Manares

Compiler: W. J. Manares

Unveiling vivid portraits of the human spirit, the anthology delves into themes of resilience, hope, and the quest for meaning. Diverse poetic forms paint a vivid tapestry that embraces readers from all walks of life. Offers solace, inspiration, and an everlasting appreciation for the enduring power of poetry. .

Book Cover Art: Kristi June

Cool Or...

kwiinmartha

Red, yellow, orange and blue
I wish I can always be with you,
Black, white, violet and pink
You are the one I always think.

I can always remember
The time we were together,
My life became colorful
It became more wonderful.

But when you turn your back on me
The time that you left me,
My life became gray
I wished you had stay.

My life becomes dark
It all becomes black,
But baby, can you come back?

For I want you back.

Colorful as rainbow
All the love that I show,
For you is true and real
For I love you still.

But when you said, "no"
My face turns into indigo,
I want to tell you
Oh, baby, please don't go.

Don't leave me crying
Don't leave me hanging,
Red, yellow orange and blue
Baby, I love you.

Black, white, violet and pink
Winning you back is what I think,
Green as the field in the farm
Baby, please come back in my arm.

Diyona Ng Bahaghari

Cherselle

Kulay ng bahaghari
May angking pangkiliti
Kaabang-abang kasi

Broken Crayons

Cherselle

My heart was shattered and torn to pieces
My ears seem to hear a million voices
Several thoughts are running through my mind
Happiness and peace, I just could not find

The world just seems to be painted in black
I cannot put my shattered pieces back
But when I saw a beautiful rainbow
Hope and joy in my heart started to flow

I remember, broken crayons' color.
I'm not done being worthy anymore
Now, I see red, orange, yellow, green, blue
Indigo, pink, gray, and violet, too.

Life might have made me a broken crayon
But broken crayons still color, and life goes on.

Colors Of Your Love

ROSEANDTULIPS31

It's yellow

And you're giving me hope and joy.

It's green

And you're inspiring me every day.

It's orange

And you're motivating my daily routines.

It's violet

And you're showing me good visions for life.

It's white

And you're respecting me as a woman.

It's black

And you're leaning on my shoulder when you're sad.

It's brown

And you're teaching me how to balance life.

It's blue

And you're taking me with my own freedom.

It's pink

And you're protecting me from many enemies.

It's red

And you're expressing your great love for me.

Kulay Ng Pag-ibig

Cherselle

Pula ang aking nakita nang magtagpo ang ating mga mata
Para bang nagsusumamong masilayan ka pa
Kahel ang kulay ng lakas nating dalawa
Kay sigla tuwing nagkakasama

Dilaw ang kulay ng kasiyahan, Sinta
Damang-dama kapag kapiling kita
Luntian ang kulay ng pag-asa,
Pag-asang hanggang huli'y tayo pa

Bughaw ang kulay ng iyong panlalamig
Yakap at halik mo'y wala nang init
Lila ang kulay ng puso kong nangungulila
Sadya bang pagmamahalan nati'y matatapos sa wala?

O, ganito bang sadya ang kulay ng pag-ibig?
Nagsimulang may init at sa dulo'y nanlalamig?
Ay, hindi na bale, magkagayunman,
Bahaghari niya'y nasilayan naman.

Hue

Kristi June

It all started black and white,

When my life was plain and out of sight.

I kept hidden in my own cave, scribbling lines, screaming pains,

Counting buses and missing trains.

There are days when people see me in a yellow dress,

Bright smile, bursting laughter, plump lips and red kisses.

They thought I was okay,

But my heart was full of gray, hiding brown blisters, mending purple bruises.

He saw me at my lowest,

Planted green seeds and pink roses,

Watered my soul with hope,

Sprinkling kindness, sweet sunshine

and sacred prayers.

Until the light at the end of the tunnel went dim,
I don't know what to do,
Northern lights turned to blue,
Midnight songs were sung, all because of you.

Makulay Na Pagkabigo

ziniriya

Ako'y pagod na—
Ako'y gustong sumuko na,
Sa bawat pagtahak ay walang saysay,
Gustong bumitaw na lang sa tuwina.
Dilaw.
Sukong-suko na sa mga pangungutya,
Palaging nahuhuli na hindi ko alintana.
Aking mga pakpak, tuluyang nabigo na.
Aking kinabukasa'y wala ng pag-asa.
Kahel.

Sinusubukan ngunit hindi na kaya,
Sinusubukan ngunit nakakasakal na.
Sinusubukan at muling ipinaglaban.
Sinusubukan nang may pananampalataya.
Abo.
Alam ng Diyos ang aking mga pagkukulang—

Datapwat, hindi niya ako kailanmang iniwan,
Bagkus ako'y kanyang ibinangon sa pagkabigo.
Inilalayan hanggang sa ako'y makatayo.
Puti.

Melancholy

Marvin Wrighttee

A haunting ghost of the past
A spirit of sorrow that lingers and lasts
A heart weighed down with its crushing despair
An emptiness that no one can repair

Thoughts shrouded in a fog of grey,
A deep sadness that won't go away
The silent screams of a heavy heart,
The pain that won't be taken apart

An eternal sadness so hard to shake,
A feeling of loss no one can take
No hope in sight to make it right,
The darkness of night, no end in sight.

Mutiny in Mt. Everest

W. J. Manares

The pink roaring siren makes my head tremble,
Oil boiling with blood in my vessel.
Roughness of the path as we travel,
The zephyr sings like a vagabond rebel.

Wet black tears under the broken buoy,
Heart as hard as a fake alloy.
Like a suffocated and cursed koi,
All aboard in a ship annoyed!

I'm a submarinated yellow titan wandering,
Redundant wonder never-ending.
Hear the deaf whales' distorted sounding,
Upon the broken hull of everlasting.

Shun the green ocean, tempt the blue tempest,
Let me see the smallest vastness,

The pirates found the perky chest,
There's a mutiny in Mt. Everest!

The Covenant Bow

Rhemaveal S. Bonifacio

Rained for forty days and forty nights,

Ark carried the second beginning of all the living,

It was dim as night, couldn't see with their sight,

Noah found grace in God's eyes, for his righteous living.

Because of man's filthiness, the heart of God is grieving,

Only eight persons and seven kinds of every paired animal seen the light,

Wonderous day! God made a covenant to the earth, rain shall come to pass,

The bow shall be seen in the cloud, the hope of the living.

Sa Iyong Piling

DManunulat

Sa bawat minuto, oras at araw na kasama kita, tila ako'y nasa gintong paraiso

Bawat ngiti mo at pagtawa tila ako'y nasa pilak na langit na.

Sa iyo, ako'y laging masaya, hindi ko ipagkakaila na mahal na mahal kita

At kung gaano ako kaswerte dahil nakilala kita.

Sa yakap mo't halik ako'y napapaimik

Sa bawat gintong sandali sa iyo ay sabik

Sa tuwing ika'y kapiling ngiti ko'y tila pilak na 'di maikukubli.

Sana'y sa habang buhay makapiling ka, makasama ka, kahit pa maraming suliranin sa buhay natin, buong puso parin kitang mamahalin.

Kapus-Palad

Haya Jhie

Kapwa ko, kapus-palad, huwag sumuko
Bukas makalawa ika'y giginhawa,
Huwag tularan mga taong basag ang pula
Kung ayaw mabansagang basang sisiw.

Hindi na bale ibon sa hukay
Lahat ng hirap na iyong pinagdaanan,
Huwag mo lamang kalimutang
Lumingon sa iyong pinanggalingan.

Lahat ay dumadaan sa hirap
May gintong kutsara sa bibig o anak-dalita,
Basta huwag lamang mag-asal hayop
Laging ikurus sa kamay ang lahat ng aral.

Kahit maging maalimuom ang kinasasadlakan
Balang araw mawawala rin ang pagdurusa,

Huwag lamang mabahag ang buntot
Tiyak na giginhawa ka rin balang araw.

Bahaghari

Christian Dave Amada

Ako'y bahagharing inimbitahan ng mundong umusbong sa langit.

Gawa sa pagtila ng ulang nagluksa sa paghihinagpis.

Nauna mang isilang ang marami at iba pang mga kulay sa himpapawid,

Ako ang higit na kilalang nakibaka sa pulang palasong akala'y matuwid.

Sa aking pag-usbong sa kaitaasan, ako ay kinutya.

Hindi tinanggap, naturingang masakit sa mata.

Malambot ang galaw, lason ang tingin, at salot para sa iba.

Hanggang sa ang simpleng balangaw, tumingkad nang husto, nangaral sa pula.

Ang pulang akala'y matwid, may agiw ang isip at lubhang makitid.

Hindi kilala ang emosyon, ganoon din ang pag-ibig.

Hindi sila 'gaya ng asul, kapayapaan ang simbolo.

Hindi 'gaya ng dilaw, pag-asa ang hatid sa pag-sikat at paglubog ng araw sa magkabilang dulo.

Ngunit sa likod ng mahabang pakikibakang ito.

Ating matatantong hindi bahaghari at pula, ang dapat magtalo.

Kung hindi ang sarado at lipas na paniniwalang itinakda ng lipunan.

Huwag ang mga kulay, kundi ang maling pagtanggap ang iyong pabulaan.

The Colors

Haya Jhie

The colors of the world are bright,
From the deep blue of the summer's night,
To the red of the rose's blush,
And the yellow of the sun's warm touch.

There's the green of the grass, the trees,
And the fields of corn, so ripe and pleasing.
The white of the clouds, so fluffy, light,
And the gray of the sky, so dark and bright.

The colors of the world are fair,
From the dark black of the night so rare,
To the silver of the moon so bright,
And the gold of the sun's warm light.

The colors of the world are free,
For all to see, for all to be.

So enjoy the colors of the world,
And let them bring you joy unfurled.

The Storm of Hope

Rhemaveal S. Bonifacio

Darkness rains, and her chaotic story will start,

In one sitting, there's a lot from the past she can't say,

Yet through the storms, she found the light that shapes her heart.

Without the white clear light, it is hard to think smart,

Even more difficult to find the right pathway,

Darkness rains, and her chaotic story will start.

Light finally becomes vivid, molding every heart,

Shedding of Christ's red blood redeem us, isn't hearsay,

God's saving grace she encountered is a work of art.

She knew she's nothing if with Christ she is apart,

Joy won't turn yellow to be shared if she doesn't pray,

Darkness rains, and her chaotic story will start.

Though it rains, she will surely find a way to start,

The black may block her way at the end of the day,

Yet through the storms, she found the light that shapes her heart.

Life and its story are truly God's work of art,

Scrubbing made colors bright, with Christ found life's true way,

Darkness rains, and her chaotic story will start,

Yet through the storms, she found the light that shapes her heart.

Panahon

Cherselle

Sa init ng dilaw na araw ay nagpagal
Hiniling na huwag magtagal
Hapding dulot ng sikat niya
Dumaloy agad ang ginhawa

Ihip ng hangin, inabangan
Dala nito'y kalamigan
Pagod ng tao'y pinapawi
Kanyang tila ba kinikiliti

Dumating din ang ulan
Minsa'y abong ambon, minsan ay itim na bagyo naman
Sana ay biyaya sa tuwina
Ngunit minsan, abala talaga

Ganito ang panahon

Iba ang bukas sa ngayon
Bawat isa'y ating pintahan
Punuin ng matingkad na kagalakan

Maaraw, mahangin, o maulan man
Tiyak na magkakaroon ng kabuluhan
Sa kamay ng Lumikha
Kagandahan at kulay ay makikita na.

Nosibalasi

Si **W. J. Manares** a.k.a Willer Jun Araneta Manares ay lumabas mula sa sinapupunan ng kanyang ina noong ika-1 ng Hunyo, taong 1985. Isang hindi-gaanong-kilalang Manunula't Manunulat. Siya ay lehitimong miyembro ng ika-7 na henerasyon ng Familia Araneta sa Pilipinas. Masaya siya sa kanyang bukod-tanging pamumuhay sa probinsiya ng Aklan - ang pinakamatandang lalawigan sa bansa. Binaliw siya ni Piers Anthony sa pamamagitan ng mga aklat niyang, "Ogre, Ogre", "Bio of an Ogre" at "But What of Earth?" at dito nagbago ang pananaw niya sa buhay. Siya ang may-akda ng mga aklat-Ukiyoto na, "Betlog", "Tanaga, Diyona... Dalit?", "Flashbacks of Flashforwards", "OTNEWUK", "Isa Sa Ilang Paraan", "Owa't Tawo", "Pusikit", "The Extracted", "Playing In Secret Solitude", "Ang Bulbul atbp." at "Poesy for Poseidon". Siya ang kusang-patnugot ng mga antolohiyang, "Magkalaguyo" at "SIIL" mula pa rin sa Ukiyoto Publishing.

Marvin Wrighttee is a writer, a poet, a singer and a programmer who crafts heartfelt verses that celebrate life's beauty and embrace its complexities. Through his words, he seeks to inspire and uplift readers, leaving a lasting impact on their hearts and minds. Marvin Wrighttee's poetry reflects his deep love for nature, human connections, and the power of imagination, creating a resonant and relatable experience for all who encounter his work.

Mary Vi Serquillos also known as **KwiinMartha** is an author from Hinigaran, Negros Occidental. She started writing last April 11, 2022. She is a Bachelor of Elementary Education Major in General Education student. An eldest and a proud daughter of a single mother. She loves to write tragic stories. She loves to watch anime and mystery movies. She prefers to stay at home and read Wattpad stories. Sunflower is her favorite flower. She loves gold and black, for gold symbolizes expensiveness and black symbolizes elegance. This is her motto: "I write not to impress, but for my feelings to be expressed".

Kristi June Sagario a.k.a. Christy Daniels is a writer, editor, singer-songwriter, client specialist, post creative strategist, educator, and a youth mentor. She is passionate about using her skills to help others. She is also a keen observer of the world around her, and she is always looking for new ideas and inspiration. She believes that the best ideas come from quick thoughts that pass in our day. Some of these thoughts turn into art, while others simply become part of who we are. As an aspiring author, she is an inspiration to those who are working to empower men and women. She is a powerful voice for change, and she is committed to creating a more equitable world for all.

Cherselle is a teacher who has a penchant for anything beautiful. She enjoys writing poems and short stories. She believes that words are alive and they bring colors to our life and our world.

Rhemaveal S. Bonifacio is known as "Avea", she's a servant of her Lord Jesus Christ and the only thing that her heart desire is to serve and glorify her God in all that she does. She is living proof that her Jesus still saves because of too many life-threatening experiences. She is a music and art enthusiast. Her hobbies are writing, sketching, crocheting, singing, planting and all that is related to music and art, she also plans to explore every medium of art and even music, because her God had put a song in her heart. She believes that life is too short to waste a second to live life another way around, because true life starts with her Jesus.

Haya Jhie is fond of writing stories about love, horror, and poetry. But she also enjoys reading meaningful books like encyclopedias, yet when you ask her, she can't answer. She enjoys dancing and singing, but singing doesn't seem to like her back. Her passion is staying at home while baking. And she dreams of becoming a renowned writer. And the quote she loves the most is: "Ang hindi marunong lumingon sa pinanggalingan ay hindi makakarating sa paroroonan".

Lovely Ruth B. Suruiz (**ROSEANDTULIPS31**), is currently a storywriter and essay writer in Wattpad, Webnovel, Dreame and Bravonovel. She is a graduate of Bachelor of Arts in Economics (AB Economics) from Ligao Community College. She pursued herself to start a journey in writing. Her first novel in year 2020 entitled, "Unanticipated Love" was written in Wattpad. Lovely is very passionate in writing so she tried to join in some writing contest online. Until now, she continues exploring her writing journey and through exploring graphic arts.

Alcel Marie A. Carbonilla (**ziniriya**) is an aspiring author from San Juan, Southern Leyte. She started writing on June 2022 and was inspired by William Shakespeare's works entitled, "Fear No More", "Romeo and Juliet," and "A Midnight Summer's

Dream". She's a Bachelor of Secondary Education Major in Science graduate and recently passed the Licensure Examination for Professional Teacher. She is a private teacher at Grace Christian Learning Center, San Juan, Southern Leyte. Alcel Marie is good at communicating with other people. She is an empathic listener and a persuasive speaker. She also uphold strong communication abilities that exhibit strong communication skills while also encouraging others to communicate.

Danica Marie Timario, manunulat at makata ng Bohol, isang bisexual. Mahigit 80 na ang naisulat gamit ang katauhan na **DManunulat**. My dalawang akda na kasalukuyang isinusulat at mababasa sa Wattpad. Mahilig sa aklat, tsokolate at kape. Ayaw niya sa pinya. Mga Taglines niya: Blood is my ink, emotion is my motivation. Let my pen express your hidden pain. Imagination is your only limitation.

Si **Christian Dave Amada** ay mula sa Narra, Palawan. Siya ay ganap na published author at EIM NC II holder. Kasalukuyang nasa ikatlong taon sa kolehiyo, kumukuha ng kursong Bachelor of Science in Social Work sa Western Philippines University – Main Campus. Taong 2019, naging pambato siya ng kanilang paaralan sa dagliang talumpati sa Division Festival of Talents (DFOT). Isa rin siya sa pambato ng Western Philippines University sa sabayang pagbigkas ft. Spoken Word Poetry sa TES congress taong 2021. Pinasok niya rin ang pagsusulat online na nilalahukan ng iba't ibang manunulat mula sa iba't ibang panig ng bansa. Doon nahasa ang kaniyang kakayahan at naging bahagi siya ng pahinang Stitches and Pen. Naging bahagi siya sa paglathala ng aklat-antolohiyang "Pagsibol: Talulot ng Pag-asa".

www.ingramcontent.com/pod-product-compliance
Lightning Source LLC
LaVergne TN
LVHW041558070526
838199LV00046B/2038